Braving the Lake

by Erin Falligant
illustrated by Arcana Studios

★ American Girl®

Published by American Girl Publishing, Inc.
Copyright © 2010 by American Girl, LLC

Questions or comments? Call 1-800-845-0005, visit our Web site at americangirl.com, or write to Customer Service, American Girl, 8400 Fairway Place, Middleton, WI 53562-0497.

10 11 12 13 14 15 NGS 10 9 8 7 6 5 4 3 2 1

Illustrated by Thu Thai at Arcana Studios

Cataloging-in-Publication Data available from the Library of Congress.

Welcome to Innerstar University! At this imaginary, one-of-a-kind school, you can live with your friends in a dorm called Brightstar House and find lots of fun ways to let your true talents shine. Your friends at Innerstar U will help you find your way through some challenging situations, too.

When you reach a page in this book that asks you to make a decision, choose carefully. The decisions you make will lead to more than 20 different endings! (*Hint:* Use a pencil to check off your choices. That way, you'll never read the same story twice.)

Want to try another ending? Read the book again—and then again. Find out what would have happened if you'd made *different* choices. Then head to www.innerstarU.com for even more book endings, games, and fun with friends.

Innerstar Guides

Every girl needs a few good friends to help her find her way. These are the friends who are always there for **you.**

Emmy

A brave girl who loves swimming and boating

Isabel

A confident girl with a funky sense of style

Riley

A good sport, on the field and off

Paige

A nature lover who leads hikes and campus cleanups

Amber

An animal lover and
a loyal friend

Neely

A creative girl who loves
dance, music, and art

Logan

A super-smart girl
who is curious about
EVERYTHING

Shelby

A kind girl who is there
for her friends—and loves
making NEW friends!

Innerstar U Campus

1. Rising Star Stables
2. Star Student Center
3. Brightstar House
4. Starlight Library
5. Sparkle Studios
6. Blue Sky Nature Center

7. Real Spirit Center
8. Five-Points Plaza
9. Starfire Lake & Boathouse
10. U-Shine Hall
11. Good Sports Center
12. Shopping Square
13. The Market
14. Morningstar Meadow

[R] emember to point your toes!" Emmy calls to you. You're perched on the diving board, overlooking the pool at the Good Sports Center. Emmy and Riley are swimming near the other end of the pool. You can't see Emmy's face through the light reflecting off the water, but you can hear the smile in her voice.

You take two steps and spring forward off the board. You try to keep your body streamlined and your toes pointed. When you hit the cool water, you open your eyes. You love the blue underworld of the pool—the bubbles swirling around you, the shadows dancing along the pool walls, and the way everything seems to move in slow motion.

When you break the surface of the water, Emmy gives you a thumbs-up. "Nice!" she says.

"Not bad!" adds Riley. Then she splashes Emmy playfully. "Ready to race?" she asks.

Riley loves a good competition, and she's a strong athlete. But Emmy's tough to beat. She swims like a fish and is a junior lifeguard at the pool. You pull yourself out of the water and take a seat to watch the race.

 Turn to the next page.

Emmy and Riley walk around to the deep end of the pool. They stand on the edge, knees bent, waiting for you to give the signal.

"Ready, set, GO!" you shout.

And they're off. Emmy and Riley dive into the water and start swimming toward you. It seems as if Riley is taking two strokes to every one of Emmy's, but Emmy's dark head is still in the lead. Just as they pass you, someone snaps the strap of your bathing suit.

"Hey!" you say, whirling around.

It's Jamie, which doesn't surprise you in the least. Her dark eyes are flashing, as they always are when she's up to no good.

"Hey, what?" Jamie says, mocking your voice. She squats down next to you. "What's going on?" she asks.

"They're racing," you mumble, nodding toward Emmy and Riley. "Well, they *were* racing."

The girls are standing together, laughing, at the edge of the pool. Riley is squeezing water out of her long blonde hair. You're about to ask who won when Jamie springs to her feet. She launches off the edge of the pool into a full-fledged cannonball, landing just a couple of feet away from the other two girls.

 Turn to page 12.

A spray of water hits your face. Emmy and Riley are sputtering, too. You can't believe how rude Jamie is being, but you're afraid to speak up and tell her to stop.

Emmy wipes her face and gives Jamie an annoyed look. "You shouldn't do that so close to us," Emmy scolds. "Someone could get hurt."

Jamie sticks out her tongue, grins, and then dives forward into an underwater somersault. She's not taking Emmy seriously, but you know better than that. Emmy never jokes around when it comes to staying safe in the water. And she's not afraid to stand up to anybody, especially when she thinks her friends are in danger. You shoot Emmy a grateful smile.

Riley grabs her towel and starts drying off. "You're such a great swimmer," she says to Emmy. "Do you think you could help me get faster? We could practice at your party on Saturday afternoon."

"Definitely!" says Emmy. Then she turns to you. "Are you coming to the party?" she asks.

Your stomach drops. You normally wouldn't miss a birthday party, especially for a good friend like Emmy. But she's having a swimming party at Starfire Lake, and that changes everything.

The truth is, you're terrified of swimming in the lake— or any body of water where you can't see the bottom. The water in the lake is green and murky. And you're not crazy about the idea of swimming with fish, turtles, and whatever else lives in that water. You shudder at the thought.

The idea of telling Emmy—brave Emmy—about your fear is almost as scary as the lake itself. You know she would never tease you about it, but you're afraid that she'll secretly think you're a big baby.

Emmy is smiling at you, waiting for an answer. What do you do?

 If you confess your fear to Emmy, turn to the next page.

 If you swallow your fear and accept the invitation to her party, turn to page 15.

If you make up an excuse for not going to the party, turn to page 16.

You respect Emmy enough to tell her the truth. You take a deep breath and say, "I want to come to your party, Emmy. I really do. It's just that . . ."

Emmy tilts her head, waiting for you to go on. "What is it?" she asks.

You look away, and the rest of your words come out in a rush. "It's the lake," you say, "the green water and the fish and the algae. All that stuff just freaks me out."

You hear Jamie snicker from behind you. Emmy quiets her with a sideways glance. Then Emmy says something you don't expect. "Lots of things freak me out, too," she says.

"Really?" you ask. You can't imagine that.

"Really," says Emmy with a warm smile. "Everyone gets scared sometimes." She's quiet for a moment, and then her face brightens. "You know, one thing that takes my mind off my fears is helping other people. I'm teaching a beginning swimming class at the lake tomorrow. Do you want to help me teach? You're a really good swimmer."

The thought of heading to the lake ties your stomach in knots, but Emmy is being so nice. And who knows? Maybe teaching other swimmers *will* help you face your fears.

"Um, okay," you say, your voice cracking. "Yeah, I guess so."

 Turn to page 28.

You can tell that Emmy *really* wants you at her party. How can you say no?

"Um, yeah," you say, swallowing the lump in your throat. "I'll be there, too."

When you see Emmy do a little happy dance, you know you made the right call. But as you walk back to your dorm room at Brightstar House, fear starts doing its own dance in your stomach. You imagine what Emmy would say if you told her how you *really* felt about swimming in the lake. She would probably say, "You can do this. Face your fears!"

As you pass through Five-Points Plaza, you spot the path that heads toward Starfire Lake. Should you go to the lake now and try to face your fears?

If you head to the lake, turn to page 18.

If you go back to Brightstar House, turn to page 22.

You tell Emmy that you can't make it to the party because you have other plans. You say the first thing that pops into your head: "I have to go home for the weekend. It's my grandma's birthday, too."

Emmy's face falls, and you instantly feel a pang of guilt.

"That's too bad," says Emmy. "The party won't be as fun without you." Then her brown eyes light up. "But you know what?" she says. "It's kind of cool that your grandma and I share a birthday!"

You smile weakly and nod, thinking, *Yeah, that would be cool, if only it were true.*

As you turn away from Emmy, your guilt is joined by another emotion—fear. Now Emmy thinks you're going home for the weekend, but you're not. How are you going to get through the weekend without getting caught and hurting Emmy with your lie?

You hurry back to Brightstar House, the residence hall where you and your friends live. You're looking for your friend Shelby, who gives great advice about things like this.

You find Shelby in her dorm room. She's working hard on a scrapbook, her dark curly hair tucked behind her ears. Shelby can tell you're upset, so she clears a space on her bed for you to sit down.

"Start from the beginning," she says.

You tell Shelby everything, starting with the moment you got the party invitation and ending with the lie you told Emmy.

Shelby's eyes grow wide with concern. She says, "Lying never turns out well—trust me. Just tell Emmy the truth. She'll understand."

You know Shelby's probably right, but her advice was so *not* what you wanted to hear. Now you're faced with an even tougher choice.

 If you decide to confess your lie to Emmy, turn to page 20.

 If you decide to hide from Emmy all weekend, turn to page 23.

You reach the lake, which actually looks calm and kind of peaceful. Nothing to worry about here, right?

A sandy beach stretches out before you. You kick off your flip-flops and take your time traipsing through the warm sand. You're half-relieved to see that there's no one sitting in the lifeguard chair. If you make a fool of yourself, you'd rather not have witnesses.

As you approach the water, your feet get heavier. You feel as if you're moving through quicksand. You can smell the lakewater now, and you can see a green layer of algae floating on the water's surface. *Ew.*

You search the shoreline for a long stick. When you find one, you swirl it around in the water, trying to clear away the muck. It works—sort of. You toss down the stick, take a deep breath, and step into the water.

The bottom is as slimy as you expected, and already, you can't see your toes. "It's okay," you tell yourself, looking straight ahead. "It's okay."

Just then, something touches your leg. It's icy cold and slippery. It wraps around your calf and won't let go.

 If you run out of the lake screaming, turn to page 24.

 If you stay in the water and try to brush the thing off your leg, turn to page 26.

The morning of the party, you wake up with a slight stomach-ache. You sit up and feel your forehead. Are you sick? You leap out of bed to grab your phone. Maybe you can call Emmy and tell her that you can't make the party because you've caught a nasty bug.

By the time you find your phone under a pile of laundry, your stomach-ache is gone. It must have been nerves. You sit down at your computer with a defeated sigh.

You decide to check the weather online. Someone said there could be rain this afternoon. Yup, there it is—a 60 percent chance of scattered showers!

You start to cheer, but then you feel that old familiar guilt. After all, this is Emmy's big day. You don't want to ruin it for her. You just want a way out of this mess.

If you hope for rain, turn to page 27.

If you hope for sunshine, turn to page 47.

You leave Brightstar House and head slowly in the direction of the pool, rehearsing what you'll say to Emmy. It's a long walk across campus. You take every chance you get to dawdle along the way.

A small footbridge passes over the stream that heads to the lake. You stand on the bridge, leaning over the rail and looking at the babbling water below. The water here looks so harmless.

Too bad it doesn't stay that way, you think to yourself. You follow the stream with your eyes until it pours into the lake beyond. You shiver and leave the bridge, hurrying toward Five-Points Plaza. From there, it's just a short walk to the pool at the Good Sports Center.

You're half-hoping Emmy won't be there anymore, but she is. You find her and Riley getting dressed in the locker room.

"What's up?" asks Emmy, smiling brightly.

"Did you forget something?" pipes up Riley. She closes her locker, turns the dial, and plops down on the wooden bench.

This is even harder than you thought it was going to be. It's a good thing you practiced your words. You stare at the ground as you tell Emmy and Riley—in a tiny little voice—the truth about the weekend and your fear.

Emmy puts her hand on your shoulder. "Everyone is afraid of something," she says gently. "But I hope you won't let that fear stop you from coming to the party and having fun."

"We don't have to swim the *whole* time," adds Riley. "We can do something else."

You really appreciate their support, and you agree to come to the party—at least for a little while. But you're still worried. How can you not swim at a *swimming* party?

 Turn to page 61.

Don't let fear stop you from having fun.

When you reach Brightstar House, you immediately search for your friend Shelby. You've got to talk to someone about this, and she's the best someone you can think of. Luckily, she's in her room.

You tell Shelby about your fear, and she's sweet about it, as always. Her hazel eyes are full of understanding.

"I'm not crazy about the swimming party, either," Shelby admits. "You know that I'm not a very good swimmer. But we can't miss the party. Just tell Emmy how you feel, and we'll figure out something else to do while we're there."

You definitely feel better after talking with Shelby, but you don't know if you're ready to confess your fear to Emmy. She's so brave. Will she understand how you feel?

 If you decide to keep hiding your fear, turn to page 19.

If you decide to talk to Emmy, turn to page 20.

It's the morning of the party, and someone's knocking at your door. You pull the covers up over your head. You've been hiding since yesterday afternoon. Why stop now?

The knocking gets louder. "I know you're in there!" calls Isabel from the other side of the door.

You groan. Isabel's a good friend, and she *does* know you're in here. You confessed everything to her on the phone last night.

You climb down the stairs, open the door a smidge, and pull Isabel inside. Her cheeks are flushed. They're nearly as red as her hair.

"There you are," Isabel says, her eyes twinkling. "I need to do some shopping for a gift for Emmy. I was hoping that you had changed your mind about the party."

You look away and shake your head "no."

Isabel is silent for a moment, and then she says, "Do you want to come shopping with me anyway? We could go in together on a gift."

You're torn. You'd love to get Emmy a gift, even if you can't go to the party. But what if someone who thinks you're visiting your grandma sees you shopping?

 If you go with Isabel to get a gift, turn to **page 40**.

 If you tell her to go on without you, turn to **page 62**.

As you race out of the water shrieking, you can hear someone calling to you. Logan is standing on the footpath that winds around the lake.

"Was it a fish?" she asks. She sounds a little *too* excited.

"I don't know," you answer, embarrassed. "And I'm not sure I want to." You examine your ankle. There's no trace of the slimy thing. You shudder with relief.

You walk the path back toward Brightstar House with Logan, and it doesn't take long before you've confessed your fears to her. Logan is one of those girls who needs to know everything—there's no point in holding back. Plus, she's awfully smart. You're hoping that maybe she can help you.

When you're done talking, Logan nods her head. "I get it," she says. "It's like my fear of being called on in class and not having the answer. I dream about it all the time."

That's *so* Logan. You can't help but smile.

"Oh, and I'm a little scared of lightning," Logan adds sheepishly, tilting her head down as if to hide behind her brown bangs. "A *lot* scared, actually."

"Really?" you say. "So how do you deal with it?"

"I try to learn more," Logan says. "The more I know about lightning, the safer I feel. Like, did you know that lightning is a lot like static electricity?"

You shake your head. You didn't know. But Logan just gave you an idea. "You're great at finding things out," you say to her. "Can you help me learn a little bit more about the lake?"

"Of course!" says Logan. "When do we start?" There's something about the enthusiasm in her voice that makes *you* feel more excited and confident, too.

"Um, right now?" you ask. "The swimming party is this weekend. There's no time like the present."

Turn to page 33.

Try to learn more. The more you know, the safer you'll feel.

You muster up the courage to reach down and brush the cold, wet thing from your leg. You fling it as far away from you as you can. You recognize it as soon as it hits the water. It's a plastic bag.

"They're everywhere," you hear a familiar voice groan. You turn around and spot Paige on the beach behind you, holding a stack of flyers and a stapler. She points toward another bag bobbing just below the pier.

You can't believe you were scared of a plastic bag. Embarrassment creeps across your face, but Paige doesn't seem to notice. She waves a flyer in your direction.

"Here, this is for you," she says.

You don't waste any time getting out of the water and sliding back into your flip-flops. "What is it?" you ask, reaching for the flyer. The headline of the flyer reads, "Save the Lake!" and there's an adorable picture of a duckling swimming along the lakeshore.

"I'm organizing a cleanup party for this Saturday morning," says Paige. "Nine o'clock."

Paige is always doing something to try to help the environment. You admire her for that.

Turn to page 30.

Your wish comes true! It's starting to rain outside. You feel relieved, but also guilty.

Just when you start thinking you're a horrible friend, Emmy pokes her head into your room. She looks awfully perky for a girl whose party is being rained out.

"Hey!" she says brightly. "I'm rescheduling my party for tomorrow. Can you come?"

It's all you can do not to burst into tears. *Here we go again*, you think.

"It's supposed to be *really* sunny and warm tomorrow," says Emmy, dashing your hopes of another rainy day.

You push away your dark thoughts and give Emmy your warmest smile. "I'll be there," you say.

You go to bed with a feeling of dread. When you wake up the next morning, that feeling is still there. But you'll go to the party. There seems to be no way around it.

Turn to page 47.

The next afternoon comes too quickly. It takes every ounce of courage you've got to head to the lake for Emmy's swimming class. When you get there, you're relieved to see your friend Shelby in the water. She seems pretty relieved to see you, too. A huge smile spreads across her face, and she waves excitedly.

Emmy is teaching Shelby and the other girls in the shallow water, which is separated from the deep water by a rope. That's good news for the girls who can't swim, but it's bad news for you. The shallow part of the lake has the slimiest bottom. You shiver.

"Come on in!" Emmy calls to you. "I was just about to demonstrate the back float. You can help!"

The back float is easy for you—at least when you're swimming in the pool. There's nothing easy about stepping into the lake, though. You look down at your feet in the sand, wondering if you can make them move.

If you take a step into the water, turn to page 34.

If you stay onshore, turn to page 31.

"What do you think?" asks Paige. "Will you help me get some of this trash out of here?"

You hesitate. "I don't know," you say. "Emmy's party is Saturday afternoon and—"

"Oh, we'll be done in plenty of time for that," says Paige. "In fact, if we can get a few more girls to help us, the clean-up should take only a couple of hours."

Paige is so enthusiastic. You don't know how to tell her that what you're really worried about isn't time—it's your state of mind. After today's lake experience, you're pretty sure that you'll be a nervous wreck by the time Saturday morning rolls around. You think saving the lake is a great idea, but you're more worried about who is going to save *you* from the lake.

 If you accept Paige's invitation, go to page 38.

 If you tell her that you'll be busy that morning getting ready for Emmy's party, go to page 19.

Emmy's waiting for you to join her in the water, but you can't move. Your feet are frozen. It feels as if there are a thousand pairs of eyes on you. The girls who are watching you don't even know how to swim, but they're still brave enough to be in the water—much braver than you.

You can feel the tears coming. You have to get out of here quickly.

"I can't—um, I just remembered this thing. There's something I was supposed to do," you stammer. You wave apologetically and then quickly turn away, nearly running into the lifeguard. She looks at you sympathetically, which makes the tears flow. You can't get out of there fast enough.

You hide out in your dorm room at Brightstar House for the rest of the day, and the next. In fact, you pretty much avoid Emmy until the day of the party. You don't know what else to do.

Turn to page 47.

You head to Starlight Library with Logan. She hops online and types in a few keywords to search for. Pictures of fish and turtles start popping up onscreen. Logan's really good at this.

"Hey, what's that?" you ask her. You lean closer to the screen to get a better look.

"A water snake," she says. "Isn't it cool?"

You shrink back and make a face.

"Oh, right," says Logan. "Fear. Let's see if we can find a book about that." She searches the library catalogue and jots down a number on a scrap of paper. "This should be in the nonfiction area."

You find the book, called *No More Fear*. As you slide it off the shelf and flip through a few pages, someone calls out, "Hey, scaredy-cat. What are you afraid of?"

It's Jamie. She's standing at the end of the aisle, staring at the cover of your book. The girl must have 20-20 vision. She's really starting to get on your nerves.

 If you speak up and answer Jamie, turn to page 57.

 If you ignore her and walk back to Logan, turn to page 36.

You hesitate for a moment, but all of the girls—including Shelby—are waiting for you. How can you not go through with this?

You walk slowly toward the water, concentrating on Shelby's smiling face. As you step into the lake, you feel mud instantly ooze up through your toes. Your foot slips forward and you wobble a bit.

One of the girls closest to you says, "I know. It's kind of like a mud bath, isn't it?"

A mud bath. That makes you giggle. You take a few more quick steps and then lower your body into the water. It's cold, but you're relieved that you can finally lift your feet up off the lake bottom.

Now that you're in the water, you're surprised to see that it's not as brown and murky as you thought it would be. Still, you're not quite ready to put your face in the water. You keep your head up and start doing the breaststroke toward Emmy.

"Hey, you're good!" calls Shelby.

That gives you a burst of confidence. You take a few strong strokes, and then you're by Emmy's side. She greets you with a big grin. She's the only girl here who knows how hard it was for you to get in the water, and you can tell she's doing a silent cheer for you. You're grateful to her for not making a big deal about all of this in front of the other girls.

"Okay," says Emmy to the other swimmers. "Let's talk about the back float."

You flip over onto your back to show the girls how it's done. You arch your back and spread your arms. While Emmy describes the back float, you take in the sky above. It's a brilliant blue. In this position, you can almost pretend you're in the clear water of the swimming pool.

You help Emmy demonstrate a few more strokes. By the end of the lesson, you're feeling pretty comfortable in the water. You start to actually look forward to the party.

 Turn to page 97.

You find Logan by the printer, gathering up pages of wildlife photos. "It'd be better if we could see these things in person," she says. Her eyes light up, which means she has a good idea.

You follow Logan back to her room at Brightstar House. She grabs an underwater camera from her bookshelf. "We'll take our own pictures," she says. "We'll see how many things we can find at the lake. It'll be just like a scavenger hunt!"

When you get to the lake, Logan spots a frog and starts snapping pictures as she splashes along the shoreline. You stay on dry land. You keep thinking about that photo of the water snake. Then you spot a newt perched on a log. Its belly is bright red.

"Hey, Logan. Check this out!" you call to her.

Logan inches out onto the log to see if she can get a shot of the newt. "Wow," she whispers, "that's a red-bellied newt. I've never seen one near the lake before. C'mon, you should see this little guy!"

⭐ If you climb onto the log with Logan, go online to innerstarU.com/secret and enter this code: URBRAVE

⭐ If you search for newts onshore, turn to page 39.

Early Saturday morning, you head to the lake. You see lots of girls carrying trash bags. You're glad to see that Paige's cleanup party is a success.

"There you are!" calls Paige. Her blonde hair is tucked beneath a hat and she's wearing a pair of work gloves. She tosses you a pair, along with a trash bag, and invites you to walk with her around the lake.

Emmy's party is just a few hours away, and your stomach is a nervous mess. As you walk with Paige, you tell her about your fear. You've got to talk to someone.

Paige is silent for a moment, a thoughtful look on her freckled face. "Want to know what I do when I'm scared?" she finally asks. "I hug a tree."

You giggle. Paige is *such* a nature girl.

"I know that sounds weird," says Paige, "but it just makes me feel stronger."

Suddenly Paige stops walking and grabs you by the arm. "*Shhh…*" she says.

Your stomach lurches. *What is it?*

 Turn to page 44.

"It's so cute!" calls Logan, just as the newt slides back into the water.

Forget the frogs. Logan's on a mission now to find more newts. No matter how much she coaxes you to join her in the shallow water, you're more content on shore.

You search the grass for newts, frogs, and other critters, but you find nothing. You decide to leave the searching to Logan. To pass the time, you pull out the book you checked out from the library.

 Turn to page 42.

You decide to go with Isabel, but only if she agrees to take the long way so that no one sees you. It takes forever to wind around the lake, but you make it to the Shopping Square without running into anyone you know.

Isabel steers you toward Girl Gear, a sports shop. As she opens the shop door, a little bell jingles overhead. You follow Isabel through the door and to the back of the shop. Clearly, she's been here before.

Isabel stops in front of a rack of beach towels. Perfect! You wonder which color Emmy would like.

You're so deep in thought that you barely hear the bell jingle again over the front door. Isabel glances up and sucks in her breath. "It's Emmy!" she whispers.

If you face Emmy, turn to page 46.

If you slip out the back door, turn to page 50.

You flip to a chapter in the book called "Top 5 Ways to Face Your Fears." That sounds like a good starting place.

You scan the list. The first piece of advice is, "Talk about your fears with friends."

Check, you think to yourself. One down, four to go.

 To read number 2 in the list, go to the next page.

 To read number 3, turn to page 54.

 To read number 4, turn to page 75.

 To read number 5, turn to page 111.

Top 5 Ways to Face Your Fears

1. Talk about your fears with friends.

"Number 2," you read out loud. "Question your fears. Ask yourself, 'What is the worst thing that could happen?'"

You close your eyes and imagine yourself walking into the lake. What's the worst thing that could happen? Suddenly, you see yourself surrounded by a school of fish with razor-sharp teeth. They dart toward you and start attacking your toes.

"Yikes," you say, slamming the book shut.

"What's wrong?" asks Logan.

You jump a little at the sound of her voice. You didn't realize she was so close to you. You describe the killer-fish scene to Logan, and she shakes her head.

"No way," says Logan. "We don't have fish like that in this lake."

Logan's probably right—she usually is. But you decide to read on.

Turn to page 54.

"Ducklings!" Paige whispers, slowly releasing her grip on your arm. She points toward the water.

A parade of ducklings is swimming along behind a mama duck, hugging the shoreline. The baby ducks bob up and down in the water. You can't remember the last time you saw something so cute.

Paige sighs. "That's why we're doing this," she says. "Did you know that ducks can get their heads stuck in those plastic rings—the ones from water-bottle packages? They're like traps for those little ducklings. It's awful."

You feel a pang in your chest. You didn't know. But you're starting to realize why Paige is so passionate about cleaning up the lake.

As you watch the ducklings disappear around a bend, you make a decision. You're doubly determined now to find every bit of trash you can along this precious lakeshore. You grab your bag and start searching the grass for pop cans, plastic bottles, and other litter.

🌟 Turn to page 52.

As Emmy walks down the aisle toward you, you realize there's no way around it—you have to face her. Emmy sees Isabel first and waves hello. Then Emmy sees you. She stops waving, and you can see the confusion in her eyes.

"Hey, weren't you going to go to your grandma's?" Emmy asks.

Your mind goes blank. You look to Isabel for help, but she seems to have crawled into the towel rack.

You hear yourself talking. It's as if someone else is controlling your mouth. "I needed to buy Grandma a gift," you say. You glance across the aisle and grab the first thing you see—a purple football.

Emmy's silence speaks louder than words. She stares at the football for a moment and then looks back at you. "Well," she says with a shrug, "I hope your grandma really likes it."

 Turn to page 60.

An hour before Emmy's party is due to start, the sun is shining brightly. You've run out of excuses, so you look in the mirror and give yourself a good talking to. You remind yourself that Emmy is your friend, someone you really like and admire. You tell yourself that you don't have to swim, but you *do* have to go to the party.

As you walk toward the lake, you see lots of bright balloons bobbing from the pier posts. Girls are laughing and splashing around in the water near the beach. You suddenly feel sick to your stomach.

Then you hear Emmy calling to you from the pier. She's helping Riley step down into a canoe. You walk toward Emmy, happy to leave the swimming area behind.

"I am *so* glad you came," Emmy says, and you can tell she really means it. "Want to join us?" she asks, nodding toward the canoe.

You're torn. You're not crazy about canoeing, but it has to beat swimming in the lake.

 If you go canoeing, turn to page 98.

 If you find a place to sit on the pier instead, turn to page 64.

You try to convince Shelby that she should go have some fun, that you'll be okay on your own. Shelby's not so sure. Then she spots some of the girls from swimming class waving at her from the water. They're all wearing life jackets—one of Emmy's rules today for beginners.

Shelby gives you one last questioning look, as if to say, *Are you sure?* You give her a thumbs-up and your biggest smile.

Shelby grabs a yellow life jacket from the pile beside the boathouse. She slides her arms through the jacket, buckles it, and then races down the beach toward the water. She steps into the water cautiously. It must be pretty cold. A shiver runs down your spine.

From your safe spot on the pier, you watch Shelby— brave Shelby—launch into the water, shrieking as she runs toward the other girls. Pretty soon she's paddling through the water with her hands. She's not a strong swimmer, but that doesn't stop her. She's pushing past her fears in order to have fun with her friends. You wish you could be more like her.

Something interrupts your thoughts. It's Jamie, shouting from deeper water. "Hey, look!" she's saying, pointing her finger. "Look at that big yellow turtle!" You turn to look. Everyone else does, too.

Your heart sinks when you realize Jamie is pointing at Shelby. Shelby's life jacket is creeping up around her ears. She *does* look sort of like a turtle with its head pulled into its shell, but Jamie shouldn't be making fun of her.

When Shelby realizes that everyone is staring at her, her face falls. You can see her hurt and embarrassment. You also see the moment when she replaces that hurt with steely determination. She's going to do her best to ignore Jamie.

"Look out for the yellow turtle!" Jamie's saying. "It might be a snapper!" It doesn't sound as if she's going to let up with the teasing thing anytime soon.

 If you decide to say something to Jamie,
turn to page 90.

 If you decide to stay silent, turn to page 66.

"I have to get out of here!" you whisper to Isabel. You look wildly around the store and spot an exit sign above the back door. You crouch down low and wind your way around clothing racks.

When you reach the back door, you push it gently, hoping you won't set off an alarm. Nothing happens. You breathe a huge sigh of relief and dart out the door onto the sidewalk behind the store.

You sprint down the sidewalk, heading back toward Five-Points Plaza. As you round the corner, you almost run smack into . . . Riley.

It takes her a moment to recognize you, and then she starts laughing. "Wow, where's the fire?" Riley asks. "And aren't you supposed to be at your grandma's?"

You can't believe your bad luck—Riley, of all people. And now she's staring at you, waiting for an answer. You see a flower stand behind Riley and tell her that you're making a quick stop on your way out of town to buy flowers for your grandma. You can't seem to stop lying.

"Great idea!" says Riley. "Maybe I'll buy some flowers for Emmy, too."

Now you're stuck. You spend a half hour looking at every bud and blossom in the flower stand. You hope that if you shop long enough, Riley will get bored and leave before you actually have to spend money on something. No such luck.

You end up blowing your allowance on a bouquet of daisies for "Grandma," and you're not sure you have enough money left over to give to Isabel for Emmy's gift.

Isabel! She's probably wondering where in the world you disappeared to.

"I have to go," you tell Riley. "Will you tell Emmy happy birthday for me?"

"Will do," says Riley. "Have fun at your grandma's!"

As you shove the daisies into your backpack, you try to shove down the guilty feelings inside you. More lies. Ugh.

You head through the Shopping Square, scanning the sidewalks for Isabel. You're grateful for her red hair. She should be easy to spot—that is, if she hasn't given up on you and gone home.

 Turn to page 56.

You spend the morning cleaning up the lake area with Paige. The two of you have filled four or five bags with trash. You can't believe how good you feel.

When you get back to the beach, you find Emmy there. She seems relieved to see you. "Can you guys help me get this canoe onshore?" she asks.

"Sure," says Paige. "But don't you want to leave it in the water for your party?"

"It looks like it's going to storm," says Emmy sadly. "I might have to postpone the party."

You've been so busy working that you didn't notice the dark clouds brewing overhead. The wind is picking up, too.

"You take these," Paige says, handing you her trash bags. "I'll help Emmy."

You set the bags at the foot of the pier, next to an over-flowing trash bin. You separate the black bags from the white ones, which are full of cans and plastic bottles to be recycled.

As you step off the pier and start walking toward the boathouse to join the other girls, something white and billowy catches your eye. A sail? No—it's one of the white trash bags skipping across the pier, caught in a gust of wind. You spot it just as it rolls off the side of the pier and splashes into the lake.

If you go into the water after the bag, turn to page 58.

If you try to reach it from the pier, turn to page 70.

"Number 3," you read to yourself. "Chase your fears." Huh? You're not sure what that one means. You read it again, this time out loud.

Logan pops her head up from the tall grass. "Chase?" she says. "Are you sure it doesn't say 'face'?"

You check the book. "*Chase* your fears," you read again carefully.

Logan thinks about that for a moment. "Oh, I get it," she says. "Have you ever had a dream that you were being chased by a monster or something?"

"Um, yeah," you say reluctantly. You don't really want to admit another fear, but you used to have monster dreams all the time when you were younger.

"Well," says Logan, "I had a dream like that once. And instead of running away, I decided to turn around and start chasing the monster. And you know what happened?"

You shake your head. You don't think you could ever be that brave, even in a dream. "What happened?" you ask.

"The monster started running away from *me*," says Logan. "Suddenly it wasn't such a big scary thing anymore. Maybe if you chase your fears, they won't seem so scary anymore either."

You nod slowly. Logan is pretty smart. But how do you "chase" your fear of swimming in the lake? You imagine yourself sprinting toward the lake, your arms pumping and your face fierce. You giggle as you picture the fish in the lake sprouting little legs and running away from you, terrified.

"What?" begs Logan when she sees you laughing. "Tell me. *Please!*" It kills her not to know what's going on inside your head.

You describe to Logan the image of the fish standing up on their legs and racing away from you. That gets Logan giggling, too. You thank her for the great advice.

 If you're ready to "chase your fear," turn to page 88.

To read about other ways to face fear, turn back to page 42.

If you chase your fears, they won't seem so scary.

You peek through the windows of Girl Gear and a few other shops, looking for Isabel. You don't see her. She must have gone back to her room at Brightstar House.

If you take the shortcut through Five-Points Plaza, you might be able to catch Isabel before she leaves for the party. But the plaza is a busy place. You might run into other girls you know, and you're still pretty shaken up after running into Emmy and Riley.

 If you take the shortcut back through Five-Points Plaza, turn to page 63.

If you take the long way back to Brightstar House, turn to page 69.

You decide to catch Jamie off guard with a joke. You motion to her to come a little closer. Then you lower your voice and say to her, "What am I scared of? The new library attendant."

You peek above a stack of books, as if looking for the attendant. Then you duck back down. "Keep your voice down," you say to Jamie. "If she catches you talking in here, there's no telling what she might do. *Seriously*."

With that, you brush past Jamie and head back toward Logan. You can feel Jamie's eyes on your back, but she says nothing. Apparently she can't find her words. You smile, satisfied.

Turn to page 36.

As you watch the trash bag topple into the lake, you think of Paige and how her face glowed with pride when she told you about the cleanup project. You think about the ducklings that live in this lake. And then you start to run.

You catch another trash bag before it spills off the pier. You cover it with the heavy lid of the trash can, and then you race to the end of the pier. The first bag is way out of reach, already spilling its contents into the water.

Standing on the edge of that pier, you feel as if you're at the swimming pool, perched on a diving board. You think of how quickly you could reach that bag if you jumped in and swam a few strokes. You wonder for just a moment what Paige would do if she were the one standing here.

"Hug a tree," you hear Paige saying.

You reach out and wrap your arms around one of the sturdy wooden posts at the end of the pier. It's no tree, but it's strong and tall. You feel a surge of strength run through your own body. You turn back to the water and—before you can talk yourself out of it—you spring into the air and plunge into the lake.

You keep your eyes closed as you hit the water. When you surface, you take a few strong strokes, imagining that you're swimming in the clear water of the pool. Pop cans and plastic bottles litter the water around you. That makes you swim faster.

The handle of the trash bag is within reach, and you lunge for it, which sends you underwater again. When you come up, you have a tight grip on the bag.

You kick your legs and start heading back toward shore, towing the bag behind you. You reach shallow water quickly, and Emmy and Paige are there to meet you.

"What happened?" Emmy asks, her eyes wide. She wades in to take the trash bag from your hands.

 Turn to page 82.

Your heart hurts as you watch Emmy leave the shop. You're pretty sure she could tell that you were lying. Will she ever forgive you?

Isabel puts her arm around you. "Do you want to go after her?" she asks.

You shake your head. You wouldn't know what to say to Emmy even if you could catch up with her.

Isabel holds up a dolphin beach towel that you know Emmy will love. "What do you think?" Isabel asks. You can tell that she's trying to distract you and make you feel better.

"It's perfect," you tell Isabel. Then you spot a snorkeling mask and flippers on the wall. You went snorkeling once in a swimming pool. It was pretty cool to see so clearly underwater. You wonder if the snorkeling gear could make the lake more fun for you, too.

If you buy the gear, you might be able to face your fears and go to Emmy's party. Then you could try to make things right with her. But the gear is expensive. If you buy it, you won't have enough money left over for Emmy's gift. What do you do?

 If you buy the snorkeling gear, turn to page 78.

 If you stick with buying Emmy's gift, turn to page 104.

The day of the party, Riley keeps her word. Instead of swimming, she organizes a game of water volleyball in the shallow part of the lake.

"Will you be on my team?" she asks you, tossing you the volleyball.

You know Riley is trying to help you, but you don't know what to say. If you agree to play, you'll have to get in the water, and it sure doesn't look very appealing.

If you play the game, turn to page 86.

If you pass, turn to page 93.

"I'm sorry," you say to Isabel. "I can't take the chance. If Emmy finds out I'm here, I'll feel awful."

Isabel touches the doorknob. Then she turns and asks, "Are you sure you can't try talking to her?"

You shake your head firmly. "I just don't think I can," you say.

Isabel sighs and gives you a sad smile as she steps out of your room.

After Isabel leaves, you watch the clock. The rest of the morning drags by like a movie played in slow motion. When it's finally time for the party to start, you feel a wave of loneliness. You don't think you can spend another minute in your room by yourself. And why should you? There's no chance of running into your friends on campus when everyone you know is at the lake.

You get dressed and walk toward the library. You should stay there, but you don't. You walk a little farther down the path toward the lake. There's a cluster of trees behind the boathouse. If you stay there, you can peek through without being seen.

There they are. You can see your friends swimming by the pier. You can hear their shrieks of laughter. You wish more than anything that you could be having fun with them, but you can't. You let your fear—and a lie or two—get the better of you.

The End

Going back through the plaza was a good decision. You don't run into anyone you know. You realize, sadly, that your friends are probably all getting ready for Emmy's party.

When you get back to Brightstar House, you knock on Isabel's door. She doesn't answer. You check your watch. It's later than you thought it was. The party is starting any minute now.

When you open your own bedroom door, you find a note on the floor from Shelby:

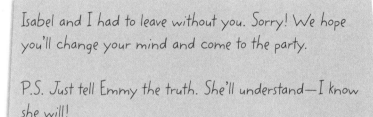

Isabel and I had to leave without you. Sorry! We hope you'll change your mind and come to the party.

P.S. Just tell Emmy the truth. She'll understand—I know she will!

 If you decide to take Shelby's advice and finally confess to Emmy, turn to page 106.

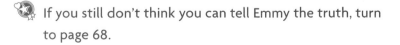 If you still don't think you can tell Emmy the truth, turn to page 68.

You find a comfortable spot on the edge of the pier, overlooking the swimming area. When Shelby sees you sitting there, she hurries over to join you.

"Did you save me a seat?" she jokes, sitting down beside you.

"Nope," you say with a smile. "You're supposed to be swimming!"

Shelby shakes her head. "I'd rather sit here with you," she says kindly. You're not sure if you believe her, but you're grateful for her company.

You see Jamie get out of the water and start walking toward the pier. You're afraid she's going to sit by you, but she doesn't. Instead, she brushes past you, saying, "Wow, you two are about as much fun as bumps on a log." Then she takes a leap off the end of the pier.

You ignore Jamie's comment—you're getting pretty good at that. You don't care what Jamie thinks, but you *do* feel bad that your fear may be holding Shelby back from having a good time.

 If you tell Shelby to go on and have fun without you, turn to page 48.

If you look for a way to have fun with her, turn to page 76.

You and Logan decide to go to Emmy's party together. When you get there, Logan hands Emmy a present—a framed picture of the tiny newt on the log. You have a photo just like it at home, a gift to you from Logan.

What you know now is that you're much braver than you thought you were. You also know that Logan was right—sometimes knowing more really *can* help you face your fears.

The End

You want to tell Jamie to knock it off, but you don't want to make things worse for Shelby by making a scene. She's still trying to ignore Jamie, but you can tell the turtle jokes are starting to get to her.

When you see Shelby take the life jacket off, you get nervous. Emmy would make Shelby keep it on, but Emmy is canoeing—too far away to notice. You scan the beach for the lifeguard and are relieved to find her there, perched high in her chair.

You remind yourself that as long as Shelby stays in the shallow water, she'll be fine. She's holding on to a big beach ball, just inside the ropes of the shallow swimming area.

When you hear a loud splash at the end of the pier, you whirl around. It's Jamie doing another one of her obnoxious cannonballs. Apparently the lifeguard has had enough of them, too, because she climbs down from her chair and walks toward Jamie.

When you glance back toward Shelby, you can't find her. Your heart starts to pound. There she is—on the other side of the ropes, reaching out for the beach ball. As she paddles the water to get to the ball, she pushes it farther away.

"Shelby, stop—" you say. But it's too late. She's gone too far, and she loses her footing on the slippery dropoff.

Turn to page 72.

You crumple up Shelby's note. You're afraid to try to set things right with Emmy. What if you end up making things worse?

You pull the daisies out of your backpack and toss them in the trash. You don't even want to look at them. They're a reminder of a horrible day.

You think about the lies you told to cover up your fear. You think about how much fun the girls must be having at the lake, without you. You curl up on your bed and finally let the tears flow.

The End

You take the lake path back toward Brightstar House, which seems like a good idea—until you realize that you'll be walking *right* past Emmy's birthday party. From this point on the path, you can already see Emmy down by the boathouse. She's tying balloons to the posts of the pier.

You duck behind the boathouse and into the trees. Instead of working your way back toward the trail, you stay put. You can't tear yourself away from the lake or shake the feeling that you should be there, celebrating with Emmy. It's especially hard knowing that you lied to her.

Standing there, hiding behind the trees, you make up your mind to tell Emmy the truth. You're afraid that if you don't, you might lose her friendship, and you care way too much about her to let that happen.

Now you just have to figure out what you'll say to Emmy—and when.

 Turn to page 106.

You run toward the pier. You kneel on the edge and try to grab the trash bag, but it's too far away. You could kick off your shoes and jump into the lake after the bag. But under these dark clouds, the water looks murkier than ever. There must be another way.

You search the shoreline for a long stick. You find one, but as you look up, a gust of wind sends two more bags bouncing off the pier. Pop cans bob in the rough water.

You call to Paige and Emmy for help. When Paige sees what has happened, her face looks as dark and stormy as the clouds above. She runs toward the pier just as the clouds break open and the rain comes pouring down.

"Paige, come back!" calls Emmy. "It's not safe!"

Paige hesitates, but a flash of lightning sends her sprinting back toward the boathouse. The three of you huddle together just inside the door.

Paige is fighting back tears. "I'm sorry that all of our hard work was for nothing," she says. She thinks you're as frustrated as she is, but what you're really feeling is guilt. You could have grabbed that first bag, if you'd been more brave. And maybe you could have stopped the others from spilling into the lake, too.

It seems as if the storm will never end. You watch through the window, waiting for the lightning to pass. When it finally does, you, Emmy, and Paige step outside into the light rain. The sky is starting to clear over the lake, and you can see—even from the boathouse—cans and bottles littering the surface of the water.

Paige walks down toward the pier, her shoulders sagging and her steps heavy. You follow her and sit with her on the end of the pier. Paige is so sad that she can hardly speak.

"We'll clean it up again," you assure Paige. "I'll help you." And you will—even if it means you have to get in the lake to do it. Today, your fear stopped you. You promise yourself that tomorrow, it won't.

The End

This time, there's no choice. You just move. You grab a life preserver off the pier and throw it into the water. You jump in after it.

The water is colder than you expected. It takes your breath away.

When you come up for air, you search the deep water for Shelby. She's not there. You start to panic. Wait, there she is! You see her head bob above the water and then go back down again. You swim faster than you knew you could, pushing the life preserver toward Shelby. The next time she comes up, you're right there.

You push the life preserver into her hands and help her pull herself up onto it. She's coughing and looks terrified.

"It's okay," you say to her. "You're going to be okay."

You tug on the rope of the life preserver and try to swim, pulling Shelby toward shallow water. You kick as hard as you can, but you don't seem to get anywhere.

When you turn toward shore, you see someone swimming toward you with powerful strokes—the lifeguard. Relief floods through your body. When she reaches you, the lifeguard grabs hold of the life preserver and starts doing the sidestroke. "I've got her," she says to you. "Let's get back to shore."

Your limbs suddenly feel as if they weigh a thousand pounds, and it's all you can do to swim back to the beach. Someone is beside you now, helping you out of the water. When you turn, you're surprised to see that it's Jamie. She doesn't meet your eyes, but she wades through the water with you until you're back on shore.

A group of your friends is gathered there. They wrap you in a towel, and you all wait together for Shelby to get back to safety, too. Jamie watches with big eyes. She doesn't say a word, but you can tell she feels awful about what happened.

You know now that you can be brave when it counts. You only wish that you had stood up for Shelby sooner.

The End

"Grandma's was great," you lie.

Emmy looks at the ground. You're pretty sure she doesn't believe you. "Well," she says, playing with the tag on her towel, "thanks for the gift. I love it. I hope your grandma liked the football, too."

You feel your cheeks flush. *A football?* Was that really the best you could come up with?

As Emmy and Riley walk away, Emmy looks over her shoulder and gives you a sad smile. You feel awful. Sure, you saved face by not showing your fear. But you're pretty sure you hurt a good friend in the process.

The End

"Number 4," you read on. "Imagine yourself overcoming your fears."

You close your eyes and search your mind for the right picture. There it is—you're doing the breaststroke across the lake. You're so graceful and confident, you look like a mermaid. The thought makes you smile.

 If you're ready to head into the water, turn to page 88.

 To read about other ways to face fears, turn back to page 42.

4. Imagine yourself overcoming your fears.

You decide there must be a way to have fun in spite of your fears. You just have to get creative. You look around the pier and spot some brightly colored swimming noodles leaning against the boathouse.

You've played with noodles plenty of times in the swimming pool. You know that if you sit in the middle of a noodle, you can float. That gives you an idea.

"Hey, Shelby," you say, reaching for your friend's hand. "I have a plan."

Shelby grins and follows you down the pier. Good ol' Shelby—she's always up for anything.

You grab an orange noodle from the stack and toss Shelby a purple one. "Are you sure?" she asks, cocking her head at you. "I thought you didn't want to swim."

"We're not going swimming," you say to her. "We're going horseback riding." Shelby giggles, and you flash her a confident smile. You hope that your confidence holds up when you actually reach the water.

When you get to the water's edge, you step out of your shoes and shorts. You're glad you wore your suit. You were awfully tempted not to.

You take a deep breath and glance over your shoulder at Shelby. She's standing right there beside you, ready to follow you in. There's no turning back now.

You get your noodle ready, and then you count to three. You rush into the lake, stepping quickly so that you can't feel the bottom. The water's cold, but you barely notice it. You're too focused on getting to deeper water.

When the water is up to your waist, you wrap your legs around the orange noodle. You tread water with your hands until you're sitting upright, perfectly balanced. One end of the noodle sticks up in front of you like a horse's head. Your feet are floating freely, and the water around you seems much clearer than you thought it would be.

I did it, you think to yourself. *I did it!* You look back at Shelby and shout, "Sea-horse ride, anyone?"

Shelby grins and grabs her noodle, running into the water to join you. Pretty soon, the two of you are having a sea-horse rodeo. You may not be the bravest girl at the lake, but you're braver than you thought you were. And you *do* know how to have fun.

The End

You decide that it's better to show up at Emmy's party with no gift than not to show up at all. You talk it over with Isabel, and she agrees. You buy the snorkeling gear, and Isabel buys the dolphin towel.

You head to the party together, but before you get to the water, you duck behind the boathouse. You pull the snorkeling gear out of your duffel bag and start suiting up. By the time Isabel is done dressing you, you look pretty ridiculous. It takes a lot of courage—and coordination—to walk down toward the lake in flippers and a mask.

Lots of girls are sitting along the pier. When they see you coming, they start laughing and pointing. Emmy is putting a canoe into the water. She looks up to see what all the commotion is about.

When you see Emmy, you wave and lift your mask. At first, you're not sure that she's happy to see you. You hurt her a lot today. But after staring at you in your crazy outfit for a few seconds, Emmy bursts out laughing.

"What are you *doing*?" she asks, jogging up the beach toward you.

"Trying to apologize," you say. You lower the mask back onto your face. It seems easier to talk about the hard stuff when Emmy can't really see you.

You sit on the beach with Emmy and tell her the whole story—how scared you are of swimming in the lake and how you were even more scared to tell her about your fear. You apologize for lying to her. That's probably the hardest part of all.

Emmy wraps her arm around you and gives you a squeeze. "It's okay," she says. "Everyone is scared of something. I'm just so glad you're here."

Then Emmy grins, her eyes shining. "I have only one question for you," she says. "Are you going to use that snorkeling gear, or are you just trying to make a fashion statement?"

 If you decide to snorkel, turn to page 84.

If you're too scared to snorkel, turn to page 89.

You talk fast, because if you stop now, you may never find the words again. You tell Riley and Emmy the whole story—about the fear and the lies. When you finish, there's a long, awkward pause. Your cheeks are so hot, you're sure they're on fire.

You can't read Emmy's expression. Is she mad? Sad? Confused?

"So . . ." Emmy finally says, "your grandma and I don't share the same birthday?"

"Um, no," you say, looking at your feet.

"And . . . instead of going home, you hid in your room for most of the weekend?" she asks.

"Yes," you say in your tiniest voice.

"And your grandma isn't really into football?" Emmy asks. This time, she sounds a little bit amused.

"No," you say. "My grandma is definitely not into football."

Then Riley jumps into the conversation. "Wow," she says. "All that lying sounds like an awful lot of work just to cover up a little bit of fear."

You nod. It *was* a lot of work. You're exhausted.

Emmy and Riley exchange a look and a smile. Emmy glances back at you and nods her head in the direction of the pool. You're relieved to see that her brown eyes are warm and forgiving.

"C'mon," she says. "We can talk about it on the way to the pool."

You don't have your towel, your flip-flops, or even your

swimming suit, but you don't care. As you follow your friends, you feel lighter and happier than you have in days. But you still feel a little bit of fear, too. You don't know if your friendships will ever be the same, but you do know this is a good first step.

The End

You don't have time to explain to Paige and Emmy what happened. The wind is threatening to blow more trash bags into the water. You've got to get them all inside.

"Help me get the bags into the boathouse!" you say. Emmy looks as if she's about to argue. She seems much more worried about you than she is about the trash.

Before Emmy can say a word, you run for the trash bags that are still piled at the foot of the pier. Paige is right there beside you. Each of you grabs a couple of white bags.

The clouds burst open as you drag the bags toward the boathouse. The downpour seems to kick Emmy into action, too. She grabs a bag in each hand and races after you. As you pull the last bag into the boathouse and shut the door, you see a crack of lightning.

You watch through the windows as the storm rages outside. Suddenly you realize just how cold and wet you are. You start to shiver.

Emmy wraps her sweatshirt around you. Paige offers you a towel. Both girls are looking at you with admiration.

"That was a really, really nice thing to do," says Paige. "Thank you."

"It was a pretty brave thing, too," adds Emmy.

You smile at your friends through your chattering teeth. For the first time in a long time, you *feel* brave. You found a way to conquer your fear—for your friends.

The End

You pull the snorkeling mask down onto your face. As you wade into the lake, you're grateful for the flippers on your feet. They're hard to walk in, but at least you don't feel the slimy lake bottom.

You bend over and press your masked face into the water. You see swirling masses of plants and a school of tiny fish. You jerk your head up at the sight.

Emmy giggles behind you. "Fish?" she says. "They're more scared of you than you are of them."

You press your face back into the water. Sure enough, the fish have cleared out. Feeling more confident, you wade farther into the lake.

You lift your feet and use your flippers to push yourself forward. With flippers on, your kicks feel extra powerful. You wonder if this is what it feels like to be a strong swimmer like Emmy.

Soon, you're snorkeling in deeper water. The water is peaceful, almost magical. It's not at all gross and scary like you'd imagined it would be.

You're half-convinced the snorkeling gear is magic, too. It helped you make amends with Emmy, and it helped you face your fear. You vow not to take off the gear for the rest of the afternoon, except to share it with a few good friends.

The End

You agree to play volleyball, and Riley invites you to serve the first ball. As you step into the lake, your feet sink down into the mud. You try not to make a face, but your feet are all you can think about.

"Zero, zero," you holler. Then you serve the ball— straight into the net.

Isabel serves from the other side. The ball arcs over the net and heads toward you. You know you'll need to take a step forward to hit it, but you're stuck in the muck. The ball lands with a splash two feet in front of you.

After that, you pretty much miss every ball that comes your way. You can't concentrate, and you can't move. You feel as if you're sinking in quicksand.

Riley doesn't seem to mind that you're playing badly and that your team is losing. She's laughing and having a good time. But you're definitely *not*.

 If you quit the game, turn to page 93.

 If you keep playing, turn to page 94.

You and Emmy walk in silence all the way back to Brightstar House. You can't shake the shame you feel for lying to her and missing her party. Emmy doesn't seem too upset with you, and you hope that the two of you can still be friends. You know, though, that it may take a good long while before she truly trusts you again.

The End

You stand up and walk toward the sandy strip of beach downshore. When you get there, you kick off your shoes and stare at the water, giving yourself a mini pep talk. *This is it*, you tell yourself. *You can do this.* You start to sprint toward the water. Just before you reach the water's edge, your feet suddenly stop moving. You honestly can't make them move—except maybe backward.

As you climb backward up the beach, Logan is by your side. "Small steps," she whispers in your ear.

"Okay," you say, your voice quivering just a little.

The next time you approach the lake, you do it slowly, one foot in front of the other. You stand in an inch of water, letting your feet get used to it, before moving in deeper. Then you feel something flit near your left foot.

 If you run out of the water, turn to page 92.

 If you stay in the water and face your fear, turn to page 96.

You're not sure you're up for snorkeling today. You feel pretty brave for having told Emmy the truth—and for wearing this ridiculous costume in front of all your friends.

You let the other girls take turns wearing the flippers and mask. You hope that one day soon, you'll find the courage to give them a try, too.

The End

You decide to stand up for Shelby. You know she'd do the same for you.

"What's wrong with turtles?" you say to Jamie. "I think they're cute." You grab another life jacket off the pier and pull it over your head. It's wet and cold, but Shelby's grateful smile reminds you that you're doing the right thing.

You have no idea how you're going to get yourself into the water until you spot a couple of inflatable rafts leaning against the pier. Every turtle needs a log, right?

You push one raft out into the water toward Shelby. You set your own raft down in shallow water and straddle it, using your hands and feet to paddle. It takes forever to paddle all the way out to Shelby, but by the time you do, you're laughing and having a blast.

Pretty soon you and Shelby are bobbing up and down on your "logs," and a couple of other girls are trying to climb aboard. Thanks to Shelby, and even Jamie, you learned a little something: it's hard to be afraid when you're having too much fun!

The End

You race out of the water, but something feels different this time. Whatever was in that water, tickling your foot, doesn't seem quite so scary. You have a big grin on your face as you run up the beach toward Logan.

"I think we should add something to that list of fear-busters," says Logan. "*Laugh* at your fears."

You giggle as you turn around and head back down toward the water.

"See?" Logan calls after you. "It works!"

 Turn to page 65.

You pull Riley aside. "I don't think I can do this," you say to her. "It's too hard for me. I'm sorry."

"Are you sure?" Riley asks. You can tell that she's really disappointed.

"I'm sure," you say sadly. You're disappointed in yourself, too. This is exactly what you were afraid would happen. You wanted to have fun with your friends, but your fear got the better of you.

You trudge slowly up the beach toward the trail. It would be so easy to leave the party now and go back to your room. But if you stay, you might find another way to have fun that *doesn't* involve the water.

 If you decide to leave the party, turn to page 110.

If you decide to stay, turn to page 108.

You want to quit, but you don't want to let Riley down. You decide to stick it out at least until the end of the game. Maybe after that, you can find someone else to take your place on the team.

After rotating a few positions, you're standing in deeper water. That scares you at first, but you realize that the lake bottom isn't nearly as goopy out here. You also realize that if you keep moving and going after the ball, you think a lot less about the water you're standing in.

Before you know it, it's game point. If your team misses this ball, the game's over. That could mean you're off the hook, but you're surprised to find that you're not ready to quit playing. You shake out your arms and legs to make sure you're ready for the ball.

Emmy is serving from the other side. She can serve overhand—and hard. *Smack!* You see her serve heading straight for the open spot between you and Riley. You lunge for the ball but lose your footing in the slippery mud. You bump the ball with one arm just before plunging into the water. Your whole head goes under. You come up shocked, drenched, and coughing.

Riley grabs your arm to help you up. She looks worried. "Are you okay?" she asks.

You wipe your face and wring the water out of your hair. "Yeah," you say. And you realize that you *are* okay. Landing face-first in the lake water wasn't so scary after all. You're more concerned about the point. "Where'd the ball go?" you ask.

Riley grins. "You sent it right back over the net," she says. "The game goes on."

You give her a high five and rotate positions. You haven't had this much fun in the water—including the pool—in a very long time. You're glad you were honest with your friends about your fear. This is one party you wouldn't have wanted to miss!

The End

You fight the instinct to run out of the water. Instead, you picture in your mind a scene that calms you down. You imagine yourself doing the breaststroke. You're rounding the pier, and you can see your friends on the other side. They're waving to you and calling you to join them.

Before you know it, you've waded into deeper water. If you were wearing a swimsuit now, you *could* swim around that pier. Maybe you will one day soon. You smile and take another step, knowing you'll get there—when you're ready.

The End

Before you know it, it's Saturday. As you walk down the path that leads to Starfire Lake, you clutch your beach towel and cross your fingers, hoping that your courage holds out.

When you get to the party, you look for Emmy. You see her canoeing in deeper water. You also see Shelby splashing around in the swimming area. She's trying to float on her back, but her feet keep sinking.

"Want some help?" you ask her, pulling your shorts down from over your swimsuit.

"Definitely," she says. "Thanks."

You shiver as you wade into the cool water. For a moment, the old fear comes back, but you kick it aside and swim toward Shelby. You flip over in the water and describe to her how you keep your body afloat.

As you're lying there, trying to keep your heels raised, you feel a sharp tug on your foot. You try to jerk your leg away, but you can't!

You kick wildly with your other foot and try to get your head out of the water so that you can see. But now whatever has a hold of you is tugging you underwater. You take a gulp of air just before your head goes under. When you open your eyes, you can almost make out the shape of . . .

 Turn to page 114.

Emmy holds the canoe steady while you step into the front end. She takes the seat in the back, and Riley squats down in the middle. You fasten your life jacket.

Emmy pushes off from the pier and guides the canoe toward deeper water. She steers with strong, sure strokes. You paddle now and then, too, feeling some of your anxiety melt away. It's actually pretty peaceful out here.

Before you know it, the canoe is in the middle of the lake. You can clearly see the trees on the other side.

"This is the perfect spot for swimming," says Riley.

What? You whirl around just in time to see her stand up and prepare to dive. Your fingers tighten on your paddle, but you can't find your words.

"Riley, sit down!" says Emmy. "You'll tip the boat!"

But it's too late. The last thing you see is Riley's shocked face before you all tumble sideways into the cold, murky water.

Turn to page 100.

In an instant, the whole world goes green. Water rushes around you, filling your nose and ears. You flail, reaching out for anything to grab. It's as if you've forgotten how to swim. You're not even sure which way is up.

Then your life jacket starts tugging you toward the water's surface. When you burst through, the sky above you is blindingly blue. You suck in air and water and start to cough and cry all at the same time.

Emmy has a strong arm around you now, and she's tugging you toward the canoe. Riley is already there, and together, they pull you onto the edge of the canoe. You try to climb back in, but the canoe tips dangerously toward the water.

"Just hang on to the edge, okay?" says Emmy. She still has a tight grip on you.

You can't speak. You can barely breathe.

"Let's get her back to shore," Emmy says to Riley.

The paddles are floating in the water around the boat. One is within your reach, but you can't seem to loosen your grip on the edge of the canoe. Your fingers are frozen—with cold or with fear? You can't tell.

Riley tosses the paddles into the canoe, and then she and Emmy start kicking the boat toward shore. By the time you reach the pier, a group of girls has gathered there. Some of the girls are giggling, but when they see the look on your face, they stop.

You can't seem to stop crying. You bite your lip, but you can barely feel it. Everything has gone numb.

The girls grab the canoe from Emmy and hold it steady alongside the pier. Emmy helps you swim beyond the canoe toward shallower water. When you can touch bottom, you stand with shaky legs. You lean on Emmy and stagger out of the water. Several girls run down to help you, but you can't even look at them.

"Let's go dry off," Emmy says, hurrying you past the other girls. She grabs a beach towel from the sand and wraps it around you. You're grateful for her help, but what you really want is to be alone.

If you follow Emmy into the boathouse, turn to page 102.

If you tell her you need some time alone, turn to page 112.

Emmy leads you to a quiet corner of the boathouse. You strip off your wet clothes down to your bathing suit. Emmy wraps you in a warm, dry towel.

"That was pretty scary, huh?" she says.

You nod and try to catch your breath. Your shoulders are still shaking from crying. You're embarrassed to be going on like this, but you can't seem to help it.

Emmy sits quietly with you until your tears start to slow. Then she tells you something you never thought you'd hear—that she has a lot of fears, too.

You're shocked. "Really?" you say, your voice squeaking. Emmy has always seemed so brave. You wonder if she's just saying this to make you feel better.

"Being brave doesn't mean having no fear," Emmy says, as if reading your mind. "It means facing your fear when you need to."

You think about that for a moment. It makes sense. But if there was ever a time when you needed to face your fear, it was the moment you fell out of that canoe. And all you could do then was cry. You start to sniffle again.

"You know what helps me?" Emmy says soothingly. "I try to do one thing every day that scares me, something that I'm a little afraid to do. That makes me feel more brave."

Emmy squeezes your hand. "Maybe you could try that, too?" she asks.

You wipe your nose on your towel. "Maybe," you sniffle. "Maybe starting tomorrow."

Emmy laughs, and you manage to smile, too. Then she offers to walk you back to your room at Brightstar House. You'd love to be in your room right now, hiding behind a closed door, but you know there are a lot of girls down at the pier who are probably worrying about you. You wonder if you can pull yourself together enough to join them.

 If you walk with Emmy, turn to page 105.

 If you decide to stay at the party a little longer, turn to page 116.

Being brave means facing your fear when you need to.

You don't want to waste money on snorkeling gear that might not even work for you. Plus, you already promised Isabel that you'd go in with her on a present for Emmy. You know Emmy will love the dolphin towel—it's a great gift.

You pay for your half of the towel and send it with Isabel to Emmy's party. Then you head back to your room and spend the rest of Saturday hiding out. It's hard to sit in your room, knowing that your friends are having fun without you, but you don't know what else to do.

On Sunday, you run into Riley and Emmy leaving Brightstar House. Emmy has her new towel draped over her shoulders. You wonder if she and Riley are heading to the lake or the pool.

Riley gives you a friendly smile, as usual. "How was your grandma's party?" she asks.

You sigh. You're tired of lying, but you wonder if it's too late to tell the truth.

 If you make up a story about your grandma's party, turn to page 74.

 If you decide to try the truth, turn to page 80.

Emmy lets the girls know that you're okay. Then you and Emmy walk slowly back to Brightstar House. It feels good to know that there are no more secrets between you. Now that Emmy knows about your fear, maybe she can help you face it. And maybe she'll tell you more about her fears, too.

Nothing seems quite so scary anymore—not with your good friend by your side.

The End

You make up your mind to talk to Emmy, but not until the party's over. You don't want to upset her in the middle of her big day.

You spend the afternoon in your room thinking about what you'll say to Emmy. When you're pretty sure that the party's over, you head to the lake. Most of the girls have gone home, but you're relieved to find Emmy kneeling on the pier.

As you step onto the pier, Emmy looks up. She says hello to you, but she's distracted. She tells you that she just lost her favorite pink bracelet.

"Where'd you lose it?" you ask, and then you giggle nervously. "Sorry. Dumb question. If you knew where you lost it, it wouldn't be lost."

"Actually, I lost it right here," says Emmy, "when I was pulling in the canoe. I thought the bracelet would float, but I don't see it."

You crouch down beside Emmy and look over the edge of the pier. *If it went under the pier, it's a goner*, you think, but you don't say that to Emmy.

Emmy must be thinking the same thing, because she sits back on her heels and sighs. "Never mind," she says. "If it turns up, it turns up." Then she looks at you as if seeing you for the first time. "Weren't you supposed to be at your grandma's today?"

Here it is—the moment of truth. You open your mouth and tell Emmy everything, just as you practiced it all afternoon. You tell her about your fear and your lies, and you apologize for not telling Emmy how you felt right away, when she first asked you about the party.

Emmy looks away from you and takes it all in. "You know," she says after a moment, "I think you're brave to tell me the truth, especially after everything that's happened."

Relief washes over you like rain. "Thanks," you say softly. "That means a lot."

There's an awkward silence. You both seem to have run out of things to say.

Emmy stands up to leave. "Are you heading back to your room?" she asks.

If you say yes and walk back with Emmy, go to page 87.

If you decide to sit here for a while, go to page 118.

You sink down in a grassy spot near the beach and decide to watch the volleyball game for a while. Just as you sit, the volleyball goes sailing over your head.

"Oh, sorry!" calls Isabel. She chases the ball past you and into the grass.

Now you've got an idea. "How about if I'm ball girl?" you call to Riley. "That way you guys can stay wet, and I can stay dry."

"You sure?" Riley asks.

You nod and smile. *This could be fun*, you think, and it is.

You're ball girl for two games. You enjoy playing out of the water more than you do playing in it. And because your friends hit the ball out of bounds *a lot*, you get plenty of playing time.

When Riley sees that you're having fun, she seems to enjoy herself more, too. You're proud of yourself for being creative and for not letting your fear stop you from having fun with friends.

The End

What's the use? you ask yourself. You just want to go home. You find your flip-flops and pretend you're going into the boathouse. Instead, you duck around the back and head for the trail that leads to Brightstar House.

You know that you should say good-bye to Emmy, but you can't face her. You'll try to explain tomorrow, if you can find the courage.

The End

By now, Logan's practically holding the book. "Number 5," she reads over your shoulder. "Take small steps toward overcoming your fears."

"Okay," Logan says, closing the book in your hands. She points toward the lake. "Let's see 'em."

"See what?" you ask her.

"Those small steps!" she says with a smile.

"Now?" you ask her. "Seriously?"

"Seriously," says Logan. "After all, there's no time like the present, remember?"

 Turn to page 88.

"W-wait," you say to Emmy, stopping her on the steps outside the boathouse. It's hard to get the words out through your tears, but you manage to ask Emmy if she can give you a minute by yourself.

"Sure," Emmy says. "Take all the time you need." You leave her standing there on the steps, watching after you. You can tell it's hard for her to let you go on alone.

You find a quiet corner in the boathouse, away from any windows. You wrap the towel tightly around you and curl up on a bench. As you sit, you try to take long, slow breaths. You keep thinking of the moment when you fell into the water. You try to push it out of your mind. You count to 100, and when you get there, you start counting all over again.

"Are you in here?" you hear someone call from the boathouse door.

You think about not answering. You still aren't ready to see anybody. Before you can make up your mind whether or not to speak, Riley pops around the corner. Her face is pale and full of concern.

"Can I talk to you for a minute?" she asks.

You want to say no, but that would be rude, and Riley is obviously really upset about what happened.

Riley takes a seat next to you on the bench. She seems to be searching for the right words. "I'm so sorry," she says finally. "I didn't know how scared you were, and I *never* should have stood up in that boat. That was a big mistake."

"It's okay," you say to Riley, relieved that you can finally speak clearly. "I'm alright."

You appreciate Riley's apology, but the truth is, *you* feel like the one who blew it. You should have just told her about your fear. Now you've embarrassed yourself in front of everyone, and you wonder if you'll ever be able to hold your head high around Riley and Emmy again.

The End

. . . *Jamie.* She lets go of your foot, and you both come up sputtering. Jamie wipes her eyes. Then she starts laughing. "Gotcha!" she says.

When you hear Jamie's laughter, you're not scared anymore. You're *mad.*

"I can't believe you just did that," you say. The words come out louder than you thought they would. A few curious girls glance your way.

"You can't believe I did what?" asks Jamie innocently. "I was just joking around."

Suddenly Shelby is standing right beside you. "Scaring someone isn't funny, Jamie," she says. "It's bullying." As she delivers the words, Shelby looks pretty fierce. You feel a rush of affection for your friend. You feel a lot stronger now, too.

You turn back to Jamie and look her straight in the eye. "It's bullying," you say, "and it's going to stop *right here.*" You speak clearly and confidently. You say the words like you mean them—and you do.

Jamie stares back at you for a long, hard moment. She glances at Shelby, too, and then looks away. "Whatever," Jamie mutters. She turns and dives into the water, heading toward the pier.

As you watch Jamie swim away, your anger starts to cool. Whatever fear you felt is gone now, too, and you're pretty sure it won't be back any time soon.

You reach out for Shelby's hand and give it a squeeze. "Are you ready to try that back float again?" you ask her.

Shelby smiles and lifts her feet, sinking just a little before pressing her belly upward and stretching out on the water's surface. She's more determined now than ever. Each time her heels sink into the water, she kicks them back up again.

"Shelby, you're doing it!" you say to her excitedly.

But Shelby already knows that. She's staring up at the blue sky, looking every bit as strong and confident as you feel inside now, too.

The End

Emmy walks with you back toward the lake. The other girls make room for you to sit along the edge of the pier.

You decide not to wait until tomorrow to do one thing that scares you. You dangle your feet over the edge of the pier toward the cool water below. You try to erase the memory of the overturned boat and focus on how you feel *right now*.

If you close your eyes, you can imagine that you're sitting on the edge of the crystal-clear pool. The thought soothes you. It's a small step, but it's enough for today. Tomorrow, you'll take another.

The End

When Emmy leaves, you take her place on the edge of the pier. You lie on your stomach and rest your chin in your hands, staring down at the green water lapping against the posts of the pier. You wonder how something that seems so peaceful could have caused so much trouble for you.

A flash of pink catches your eye in the water below. Is it a fish? A worm? You grimace and inch away from the edge.

Curiosity gets the best of you, though, and you ease your chest past the edge of the pier so that you can get a better look.

There it is, bobbing against a post—a pink bracelet! You try to grab it, but it's just out of reach. You think about heading back to shore to find a long stick, but you're afraid to take your eyes off the bracelet. What if it floats beneath the pier?

You watch the bracelet for a long time before you make up your mind. There's only one way to get it.

You kick off your shoes and turn your body around on the edge of the pier. You slide your legs slowly into the cool water, bracing your upper body against the pier. You lower yourself down, further and further, until you're shoulder-deep in the water.

Keeping one hand on the edge of the pier, you reach your other hand toward the bracelet. When you can feel the plastic in your fingertips, you grab on tight. Got it! You reach up and set the bracelet safely on the edge of the pier.

You try to pull yourself back up onto the pier, but your arms are shaky. Instead, you use your hands to shimmy yourself along the edge of the pier. When your feet finally touch bottom, you let go and wade out of the water onto dry land.

The walk back to Brightstar House in your soaking-wet clothes is a little embarrassing. You get plenty of odd looks from girls who pass you on the path. But as you clutch the bracelet in your hand, you know it was all worth it. You found Emmy's bracelet, and you found your courage, too.

You picture the look on Emmy's face when you return the bracelet to her. It's a small thing, but maybe it will help set things right between you. All you can do is hope.

The End